LUCY TRIES BASEBALL

written by
Lisa Bowes

illustrated by
James Hearne

ORCA BOOK PUBLISHERS

It's a day at the park.
Let's be **active** today.

Playing catch is a game
our whole family can play!

"We'll **toss** nice and close.

I'll get down on one knee.

Squeeze your hand 'round the ball—
concentration is key."

"Lucy, come join our **team!**
Coach Al is my name.

I'll teach you the basics
and a love of the game!"

"Here is your **uniform,**

in the colors
you love.

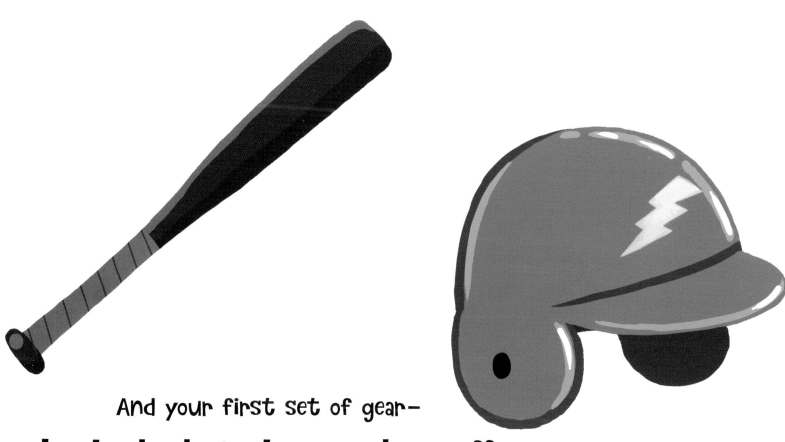

And your first set of gear—

bat, helmet and glove."

"Now stack them in a pile.
We'll go for a run.

It's called Catch the Coach.
Warm-ups can be fun!"

"Let's try some hitting.
Get a grip on your bat.
Keep your eye on the ball.
Step and swing, that's it–"
crack!

"Fielding is next,
a key skill in our sport.

Catching fly balls and **grounders**

gives
defensive support."

"OKAY, LET'S PLAY BALL!
I'll pitch from the hill."

Tom hits a chopper.
He's on base—
what a thrill!

She's afraid to stand in and get **hit** by a **pitch.**

The ball comes in fast—
it's a **SWING** and a **miss!**

Lucy takes a deep breath
and counts 1...2...3.

She's **calm** and **relaxed,**
the best way to be.

Lucy makes contact—
line drive to the gap!

Lucy **sprints** around first. Can Tom beat the **throw?**

He looks to
the base coach
**who signals
to go!**

He's heading for **home.** It's a **play at the plate!**

The catcher is ready...
Here it comes–**"Heeee's SAFE!"**

"I'm going to love **baseball!**"
Lucy knows right away.

With family or teammates,
it's so fun to play!

FAST FACTS!

Defensive Support—The players positioned out in the field are referred to as the defense. Their goal is to prevent the offense (the players at bat) from getting on base and scoring runs.

Chopper—A ball hit into the dirt directly in front of home plate, causing it to bounce high into the air. It can also be a ball that bounces many times before being picked up.

The Gap—The area in the outfield between the outfielders. The two main gaps are between the left fielder and center fielder and the right fielder and center fielder.

Challenger Baseball—An adaptive program that creates opportunities for people with cognitive and/or physical disabilities to play organized baseball.

Little League Baseball—Founded in 1939 by Carl Stotz, Little League is for kids age 4 to 16. It also includes softball and Challenger divisions. The Little League World Series takes place every summer in South Williamsport, Pennsylvania.

For every child who is trying so hard to learn new things. —L.B.

For Paula and Vicky. —J.H.

Text copyright © Lisa Bowes 2023
Illustrations copyright © James Hearne 2023

Published in Canada and the United States in 2023 by Orca Book Publishers.
orcabook.com

Library and Archives Canada Cataloguing in Publication

Title: Lucy tries baseball / written by Lisa Bowes; illustrated by James Hearne.
Names: Bowes, Lisa, author. | Hearne, James, 1972- illustrator.
Series: Bowes, Lisa. Lucy tries sports ; 6.
Description: Series statement: Lucy tries sports ; 6
Identifiers: Canadiana (print) 20220239401 | Canadiana (ebook) 20220239363 | ISBN 9781459834941 (softcover) | ISBN 9781459834958 (PDF) | ISBN 9781459834965 (EPUB)
Classification: LCC PS8603.O9758 L823 2023 | DDC jC813/.6—dc23

Library of Congress Control Number: 2022938050

Also available as *Lucy joue au baseball*, a French-language picture book (ISBN 9781459834972), and *Lucy juega al béisbol*, a Spanish-language picture book (ISBN 9781459835009).

Summary: In this picture book Lucy and her friends learn the basics of baseball, including catching, hitting and fielding, then try their new skills in a real game.

Orca Book Publishers is committed to reducing the consumption of nonrenewable resources in the production of our books. We make every effort to use materials that support a sustainable future.

Orca Book Publishers gratefully acknowledges the support for its publishing programs provided by the following agencies: the Government of Canada, the Canada Council for the Arts and the Province of British Columbia through the BC Arts Council and the Book Publishing Tax Credit.

Cover and interior artwork by James Hearne
Edited by Vanessa McCumber

Printed and bound in South Korea.

26 25 24 23 • 1 2 3 4

The author acknowledges and thanks Al Price (bigalbaseball.com) for his expertise and support.